This book belongs to:

_____

_____

_____

Copyright © 2011 by Lucy Cousins
Lucy Cousins font copyright © 2011 by Lucy Cousins

Maisy™. Maisy is a registered trademark of Walker Books Ltd., London.

First U.S. paperback edition 2014

Library of Congress Catalog Card Number 2010040144

ISBN 978-0-7636-5327-9 (hardcover)
ISBN 978-0-7636-6834-1 (paperback)

14 15 16 17 18 19 SCP 10 9 8 7 6 5 4 3 2 1

Printed in Humen, Dongguan, China

This book was typeset in Lucy Cousins.
The illustrations were done in gouache.

Candlewick Press
99 Dover Street
Somerville, Massachusetts 02144

visit us at www.candlewick.com

3 2872 50102 1442

Maisy Goes
to the City

Lucy Cousins

CANDLEWICK PRESS

Today, Maisy and Charley
are visiting their friend
Dotty in the city.

Dotty is waiting for them at the bus station. "Welcome!" she calls.

The street outside the station is really busy.
BROOM, VROOM, BEEP!

The sidewalks are crowded, so Maisy, Charley, and Dotty have to walk slowly.

There are lots and
LOTS of shops.

"Come and see the toy store," Dotty says. "It's huge!"

When the walk signal flashes, it's safe to cross the street.

The toys are *fabulous!*
Charley wants to play
with them all.

Maisy sees one to give to Dotty
as a present.

She pays for it, but— oh dear!— where are the others now?

"Are you lost?" Suddenly Maisy wishes she was safe at home.

Peacock makes
an announcement
on the intercom.

"There you are,
Maisy!" Dotty
holds her friend's
hand tight.

Then it's time to eat!
Dotty brings them
to a café in a square.

A guitarist plays music while the friends share a pizza.

Afterward, they play.
Even the park is busy in
the city!

To get to Dotty's apartment, they need to take a subway train.

"Our stop's on the blue line," Dotty says.

They squish into the subway car.

Hang on tight, everyone!

"Thank you," says Maisy.
"It's been a lovely day."

Outside, it's nearly dark.

The city lights
are bright and busy.

The stars are shining too.
They'll go twinkle,
twinkle, twinkle
all night long.